Ruby's Rainbow

Grosset & Dunlap
An Imprint of Penguin Group (USA) Inc.

Based upon the animated series *Max & Ruby*
A Nelvana Limited production © 2002–2003.

Max & Ruby™ and © Rosemary Wells. Licensed by Nelvana Limited NELVANA™ Nelvana Limited. CORUS™ Corus Entertainment Inc. All Rights Reserved. Used under license by Penguin Young Readers Group. Published in 2012 by Grosset & Dunlap, a division of Penguin Young Readers Group, 345 Hudson Street, New York, New York 10014. GROSSET & DUNLAP is a trademark of Penguin Group (USA) Inc. Manufactured in China.

ISBN 978-0-448-45863-2   10 9 8

"Max, Grandma is coming over," said Max's sister, Ruby. "Let's paint rainbows for her! Here are a smock and a beret."

"Outside!" said Max.

"No, Max," said Ruby. "You can't go outside. It's raining."

Ruby began her painting.
"What's the first color in a rainbow?" Ruby asked herself.

"Max, do you know?" said Ruby.
But Max was sneaking away to the kitchen.

In the kitchen, Max put on his red boots.

"Max? Where are you?" said Ruby.
Max was not in the living room.

Ruby found Max in the kitchen.

"Going outside!" said Max.

"No, Max," said Ruby. "You can't go outside. It's still raining. But look! Your boots are red, the first color of the rainbow! Come and paint, Max."

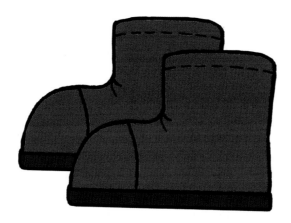

Back in the living room, Ruby made a big, red arc on her paper.

"Beautiful!" she said.

"Max, how are you doing with your painting?" said Ruby.
But Max was not there.

Ruby found Max in the kitchen again. He had taken off his beret and put on his rain hat.

"Going out!" said Max.

"No, Max," said Ruby. "You can't go outside. It's still raining. But look! Your rain hat is orange, the second color of the rainbow! Let's go back to our paintings, Max."

Ruby continued to paint her rainbow. She made
an orange arc under the red one.

"Beautiful!" said Ruby. "Max, how's your painting coming along?"
But Max was not there.

Ruby found Max in the kitchen again. He had taken off his smock and put on his yellow raincoat.

"Going out now!" Max said.

"You can't go outside, Max. It's still raining. But look! Your raincoat is yellow!" said Ruby. "Yellow comes after orange in the rainbow. Let's finish our rainbow paintings."

Back in the living room, Ruby painted a yellow arc under the orange one.

"What color is next?" she said.

"Max?" said Ruby.
But Max was not there.

Ruby went outside to look for Max.

He was in the backyard. He was wearing his red boots, orange hat, and yellow raincoat.

"Max," said Ruby. "You can't play outside in the rain!"

But the rain had almost stopped.
"Look!" said Max.
In the sky, there was a beautiful rainbow.
"A real rainbow!" said Ruby. "Green, blue, dark blue, and purple! The next colors for my rainbow! Come on, Max. Let's go finish our paintings for Grandma."

A little while later, Grandma came over. Max and Ruby each had a rainbow painting for her.

"Rainbows!" said Max.

"Beautiful!" said Grandma. "You got the colors just right."